Woosh!

W9-ATR-154

Retold by
June Melser and Joy Cowley

FRANKLIN PIERCE
COLLEGE LIBRARY
RINDGE, N.H. 03461

I had a little rooster.
I fed him on dough.

2

He got so fat
That he could not crow.

I had a little dog.
His name was Dandy.

His tail was long,
And his legs were bandy.

I had a little donkey.
His name was Jay.

I pulled his tail
To hear him bray.

I had a little donkey.
His name was Mick.

8

I pulled his tail
To see him kick.

That little donkey
Kicked so high,

I went right up
And touched the sky.

I had a little billy-goat.
His name was Toot.

He chewed my
washing,
And he chewed
my boot.

I had a little horse.
He was made of hay.

A big wind came
And blew him away.